The Town of No

Also by Wesley McNair

The Faces of Americans in 1853 (1983)

The Town of No

POEMS BY

Wesley McNair

DAVID R. GODINE, PUBLISHER
Boston

For Diane

First published in 1989 by
David R. Godine, Publisher, Inc.
Horticultural Hall
300 Massachusetts Avenue
Boston, Massachusetts 02115

Library of Congress Cataloging-in-Publication Data

McNair, Wesley.
  The Town of No.
  I: Title.
PS3563.C388T6 1988   811'.54   88-45287
ISBN 0-87923-759-7
ISBN 0-87923-760-0 (pbk)

First Edition
Printed in the United States of America

Grateful acknowledgment is made to the following publications for poems or versions of poems which have appeared in them:.

Green House: "To My Father, Dying in a Supermarket", *Harvard Magazine*: "Beggars"; "The Thin Man"; "The Visit", *The Iowa Review*: "The Longing of the Feet", *Ironwood*: "When Paul Flew Away", *The Kenyon Review*: "Ghosts"; "The Hand"; "The Name"; "Seeing Cooch"; "What It Is", *New England Review/Bread Loaf Quarterly*: "Killing the Animals", *Ploughshares*: "The Fat People of the Old Days", *The Reaper*: "String", *Three Rivers Poetry Journal*: "The Before People"; "The Minister's Death"; "My Brother Inside the Revolving Doors", *Yankee*: "The Shooting."

"The Last Time Shorty Towers Fetched the Cows"; "The Abandonment"; © 1984 by Wesley McNair, were first published in *The Atlantic Monthly*, April 1984.

"Remembering Aprons"; "Mute"; "Big Cars"; "The Fat Enter Heaven"; "The Faith Healer"; "The Portuguese Dictionary"; "After My Stepfather's Death"; "The Revival"; "The Man with the Radios"; originally appeared in *Poetry* © 1982, 1984, 1987, and 1988 by the Modern Poetry Association.

"Mina Bell's Cows"; "The Bald Spot"; "Hair on Television"; "The Thugs of Old Comics" appeared in *The Faces of Americans in 1853*, © 1983 by Wesley McNair.

"Big Cars" was reprinted in *The Anthology of Magazine Verse & Yearbook of American Poetry* (Monitor Book Company, 1985) and in *American Classic* (SCOP Publications, Inc., 1985). "Mute" was reprinted in *The Pushcart Prize X: Best of the Small Presses* (Pushcart Press, 1985–86). "Mina Bell's Cows" was reprinted in *To Read Literature: Fiction, Poetry, Drama* (Holt, Rinehart and Winston, 1987). "Hair on Television" was reprinted in *Earth, Air, Fire & Water* (Harper & Row, 1989).

I am grateful to the John Simon Guggenheim Memorial Foundation for the fellowship which helped me to complete this book. I also wish to thank Donald Hall, whose criticism and encouragement have been indispensable to this book and to me as a poet. I am indebted to Robert Begiebing, Sacvan Bercovitch, Thomas Biuso, James Cox and Mike Pride for their generous support.

"The Hand" is for Malcolm; "Where Are the Quelches" is for Ruth; "The Longing of the Feet" is for Aaron and Bill; "When Paul Flew Away" is for Paul.

Contents

The Town of No

I came as census-taker to the waste
To count the people in it . . .
I found no people that dared show themselves,
None not in hiding from the outward eye.

"The Census-Taker," ROBERT FROST

I.

MUTE

The Last Time Shorty Towers Fetched the Cows

In the only story we have
of Shorty Towers, it is five o'clock
and he is dead drunk on his roof
deciding to fetch the cows. How
he got in this condition, shingling
all afternoon, is what the son-in-law,
the one who made the back pasture
into a golf course, can't figure out. So,
with an expression somewhere between shock
and recognition, he just watches Shorty
pull himself up to his not-so-
full height, square his shoulders,
and sigh that small sigh as if caught
once again in an invisible swarm
of bees. Let us imagine, in that moment
just before he turns to the roof's edge
and the abrupt end of the joke
which is all anyone thought to remember
of his life, Shorty is listening
to what seems to be the voice
of a lost heifer, just breaking
upward. And let us think that when he walks
with such odd purpose down that hill
jagged with shingles, he suddenly feels it
open into the wide, incredibly green
meadow where all the cows are.

Remembering Aprons

Who recalls the darkness
of your other life,
sewn shut

around feed grain,
or remembers your release
to join your sisters,

the dishcloths, now
ampleness and holes?
Not the absent hands

which tied you
behind the back,
already forgetting.

How thoughtlessly
they used you,
old stove-gloves,

soft baskets
for tomatoes, and yet
how wonderfully

such being
left out
shows your inclusion!

Oh tough dresses
without closets,
lovely petticoats that flashed

beneath the frayed
hemlines of barncoats
all over Vermont.

The Hand

Her small life as a daughter
and sister and aunt

was a story of hands, the one
which they knew her by,

high up at her side
like a fin,

the other which looked like theirs,
so nobody saw it

find by itself the strings
of her apron,

or lift eggs out of a nest
between fingers,

or loosen and close
the west window

in dusk, its palm pressed
to the vanishing glass.

The Shooting

There are no photographs
of the two farmhands,
each born on the other's
birthday, with the same face.

There is no story
of why whatever
it was held them together,
closer than brothers,

broke on that day.
Only the memory
of him, the quiet one,
whispering the words

of the other
before they were said.
Only that after they
found him, holding the face

that looked like his,
and called his name
over and over, they never
mistook which one he was.

Killing the Animals

The chickens cannot
find their heads
though they search for them,
falling in the grass.

And the great bulls
remain on their knees,
unable to remember
how to stand.

The goats cannot find their voices.
They run quickly
on their sides,
watching the sky.

The Name

At the end of her life,
when the fire
lifted her house away,
and her left side
vanished in a stroke,
and she woke
in that white room
without apron or shoes;
she searched each face,
including his,
until she found her twice-
divorced daughter, the one
she'd always said wasn't
over Fool's Hill yet,
and, taking her hand
as if they'd all along
been close, began
to call the name
the frightened daughter
never heard before,
not father or brother.

Mina Bell's Cows

O where are Mina Bell's cows who gave no milk
and grazed on her dead husband's farm?
Each day she walked with them into the field,
loving their swayback dreaminess more
than the quickness of any dog or chicken.
Each night she brought them grain in the dim barn,
holding their breath in her hands.
O when the lightning struck Daisy and Bets,
her son dug such great holes in the yard
she could not bear to watch him.
And when the baby, April, growing old
and wayward, fell down the hay chute,
Mina just sat in the kitchen, crying, "Ape,
Ape," as if she called all three cows,
her walleyed girls who never would come home.

Mute

_____

Once, on the last ice-hauling,
the sled went through the surface
of the frozen pond,
pulling the son under
the thrashing hooves
of horses. Listening for him

after all her tears was perhaps
what drew the mother
into that silence. Long afternoons
she sat with the daughter,
speaking in the sign language
they invented together,
going deaf to the world.

How, exactly, did they touch
their mouths? What was the thought
of the old man on the porch
growing so drunk by nightfall
he could not hear
mosquitoes in his ears?

There is so much no one remembers
about the farm where sound,
even the bawling of the unmilked cows,
came to a stop. Even the man's name,

which neighbors must have spoken
passing by in twilight, on their way
to forgetting it forever.

II.

THE BEFORE PEOPLE

Where Are the Quelches?

O what has happened to Quelch?
Where is his great belly

and cigarette-pack breast, and where
is the thin wife who burped

spaghetti each night out
of the can, and gave such parties

the women shrieked through the wall,
the men rained urine over

and over, and the fist
of the gramophone fell asleep

unwinding the lovesick voice
of Gene Autrey. Where are the Quelches

and what do they have to do
with this shy, stooped man

shaking my hand and this woman,
so precisely speaking their names?

The Before People

There is a moment when they turn
to the ads that are meant for them
and are happy, a moment when the fat woman
thinks of melting her body away in seven days,
and the shut-in imagines big money
without leaving his home. Slowly,
as if for the first time, they read
the italics of their deepest wishes:
Made $5,000 in first month,
Used to call me Fatty, and all
the people with no confidence,
no breasts, or hair in the wrong places,
find pictures of the amazing results
in their own states. They have overlooked
the new techniques and the research
of doctors in Germany, they know that now,
suddenly so pleased they can hardly
remember being sad in this, their moment,
before, just before they lie back on the beds
in their small rooms and think about how foolish
they are or how farfetched it is or anything
except the actual photographs of their dreams.

Big Cars

Ten years later
they arrive on the thruway,
pulling winged fenders and smiling
a lane wide—big cars,
old floats that took a wrong
corner somewhere and lost
the American dream parade. Around them

the strange, grilleless
cars of the future
hum at their tires—tiny aliens
of a planet out of gas.

To think of their long trip
just beginning—the irrepressible fuel
rising everywhere into their tanks!
For the first time, armrests
unfolded out of seats;
out of the armrests, ashtrays!
Maps fell open to the new roads

which led them, finally, here
to the right lanes of America—
the antiques of optimism
nobody understands or wants
except the poor. Or dictators

driving down boulevards in some country
where the poor do not have cars
and run alongside until it seems
that they themselves are riding
on soft shocks, under a sun roof,
toward the great plenty of the New World.

Beggars

---

the one without legs reaches
up as if he would have us pull him
out of the sidewalk

we cannot pull him
our money will not help
the big-chested man whose legs
are folded in front of him
like socks

when we turn an old man
is making an earnest expression
with half of his face
two sisters remember songs
behind their white eyes

where do beggars go when the streets
are full of rain
the man in a cart rowing
his half-body away
with his hands

the girl on wood crutches
doing her slow breaststroke
into our dreams

The Bald Spot

It nods
behind me
as I speak
at the meeting.

All night
while I sleep
it stares
into the dark.

The bald spot
is bored.
Tired of waiting
in the office,

sick of following me
into sex.
It traces
and retraces

itself,
dreaming
the shape
of worlds

beyond its world.
Far away
it hears the laughter
of my colleagues,

the swift sure
sound of my voice.
The bald spot
says nothing.

It peers
out from hair
like the face
of a doomed man

going blanker
and blanker,
walking backwards
into my life.

Hair on Television

On the soap opera the doctor
explains to the young woman with cancer
that each day is beautiful.

Hair lifts from their heads
like clouds, like something to eat.

It is the hair of the married couple
getting in touch with their real feelings for the first
time on the talk show,

the hair of young people on the beach
drinking Cokes and falling in love.

And the man who took the laxative and waters his garden
next day with the hose wears the hair

so dark and wavy even his grandchildren are amazed,
and the woman who never dreamed tampons
could be so convenient wears it.

For the hair is changing people's lives.
It is growing like wheat above the faces

of game show contestants opening the doors
of new convertibles, of prominent businessmen opening
their hearts to Christ, and it is growing

straight back from the foreheads of vitamin experts,
detergent and dog food experts
helping ordinary housewives discover

how to be healthier, get clothes cleaner
and serve dogs meals they love in the hair.

And over and over on television the housewives,
and the news teams bringing all the news faster
and faster, and the new breed of cops winning the fight

against crime are smiling, pleased to be at their best,
proud to be among the literally millions of Americans

everywhere who have tried the hair, compared the hair
and will never go back to life before the active,
the caring, the successful, the incredible hair.

The Thugs of Old Comics

At first the job is a cinch like
they said. They manage to get the bank teller
a couple of times in the head and blow the vault door
   so high
it never comes down. Money bags line the shelves
inside like groceries. They are rich, richer
than they can believe. Above his purple suit the boss
is grinning half outside of his face.
Two goons are taking the dough in their arms
like their first women. For a minute nobody sees
the little thug with the beanie is sweating drops
the size of hot dogs and pointing
straight up. There is a blue man flying
down through the skylight and landing with his arms
crossed. They exhale their astonishment
into small balloons. "What the," they say,
"What the," watching their bullets drop
off his chest over and over. Soon he begins to talk
about the fight against evil, beating them
   half to death
with his fists. Soon they are picking themselves up
from the floor of the prison. Out the window Superman
is just clearing a tall building and couldn't care less
when they shout his name through the bars.
   "We're trapped!
We got no chance!" they say, tightening their teeth,

thinking, like you, how it always gets down
to the same old shit: no fun, no dough,
no power to rise out of their bodies.

The Fat Enter Heaven

It is understood, with the clarity possible only
in heaven, that none have loved food
better than these. Angels gather to admire
their small mouths and their arms, round
as the fenders of Hudson Hornets. In their past
they have been among the world's most meek,
the farm boy who lived with his mother,
the grade-school teacher who led the flag salute
with expression, day after day. Now
their commonplace lives, the guilt about weight,
the ridicule fade and disappear.
They come to the table arrayed with perfect food,
shedding their belts and girdles for the last time.
Here, where fat itself is heavenly,
they fill their plates and float upon the sky.

The Fat People of the Old Days

Oddly, being so large
gave them a sense
of possibility.

Women with huge upper arms
felt freer.

Children never stopped opening
the landscapes of flesh
which grew in their hands.

The few thin ones
were called "chinless"
because their chins seemed
indistinguishable from their necks.

No one knows when the thin ones
began to seem beautiful,
when the fat people first worried
about weight.

A woman came to fear
her elbows and knees
were sinking into dimples.

A man believed his chin,
which shook when he talked,
was also speaking.

For many years the fat life continued.

Each day inside strange
houses with wide doors,
fathers rose folding themselves
into their pants.

Each night the families
dreamed of bones
hung forever in fat's
locked closet.

III.

GHOSTS

The Thin Man

Once in a mirror
as it folded hair
back from its face

he discovered his eyes
earnest, lonely.
This was the beginning

of his life
inside the body,
of standing deep in the legs

of it,
held
in its elbowless arms.

And when it walked
he walked,
and when it slept

he dreamed of drowning
under its lakes
of skin.

Oh the thin man
trying to get out
learned of its great

locked breasts,
its seamless chin,
the dead ends

of its hands.
And oh the heavy body
took him

to tables
of food,
and took him down

into the groaning
carnal bed.
The pitiless body took him

to a mirror
which showed
the eyes

in a face
immense and dying,
who he was.

The Longing of the Feet

At first the crawling
child makes his whole body
a foot.

One day, dazed
as if by memory,
he pulls himself up,

discovering, suddenly,
that the feet
are for carrying

hands. He is so
happy he cannot stop
taking the hands

from room to room,
learning the names
of everything he wants.

This lasts for many years
until the feet,
no longer fast enough,

lie forgotten, say,
in the office
under a desk. Above them

the rest of the body,
where the child
has come to live,

is sending its voice
hundreds of miles
through a machine.

Left to themselves
over and over,
the feet sleep,

awakening
one day
beyond the dead

conversation of the mind
and the hands.
Mute in their shoes,

your shoes
and mine,
they wait,

longing only to stand
the body
and take it

into its low,
mysterious flight
along the earth.

The Faith Healer

When I turned,
it was like the father
had been walking right
toward me forever
with his eyes shut
pushing that boy,
all washed up and
dressed up and riding
above those long spokes
shooting light like
he was something more than arms
and a chest. Already
the mother was saying please,
oh please, partly to me,
partly because she heard
the sound, so soft
and far off at first
you might have never guessed it
was going to be the father
with his eyes shut, screaming.
But I knew, and I knew
even before it stopped
and he began to point
down at his son's
steel feet and whatever
was inside the dead
balloons of his pants,

the father did it. So when
he said he did it,
I was thinking of how
only his mouth was moving
in his shut face like
he had gone somewhere
outside of his body
which he could not stand.
And when he said
he did it because his son
burned the new barn down
to the ground, then shook
and shook so you could see
he was inside his body
and could never leave,
all I could think
was how the wind was moving
the tent. Lifting it up
and up around the father
who could not see it lifting,
and the mother with the no–
color dress, and that small,
still boy, all washed up
and dressed up and
looking right at me
almost like it was OK
being a chest. Which was the moment

when my own legs went out
from under me, and I woke
with the cold steel bars
of his wheelchair fast
in my hands, and shouting
like for the first
time, *heal, oh heal,*
over and over to the legs
that could not walk,
and to the legs
that could, and to everyone,
everywhere, who could never
get free from such sadness.

The Portuguese Dictionary

Each morning Charley
the house painter
came to work, he left
his clenched face
holding its unlit
cigar, and his old hands
moving in their dream
of painting pastel colors
on new houses that stood
in cow pastures. He
was selling sewing machines
in Brazil, just as if
thirty-five years
had never happened. This
was why each afternoon
he looked right through
the baffled landowners,
come to imagine
their twiggy sticks
would soon be trees.
Why when he got home
he never even saw
his wagging, black
habit of a farm dog,
or thought about his mother
nodding in the far room
among the water-stained

explosions of roses. Already
Charley was at his desk
down in the cellar,
waiting for his slow
legs and hands to come
and get the index cards
out from the shelves of dead
pickles and jams. Already
he was thinking
of the name for sky
with no clouds in it.
Or of the happy words
the women of Brazil said,
working the treadle.
Or of the lovely
language of the face
and legs and hands he learned
from a boy one night
beside the dark sea,
in some other life
of his lost body.

Breath

Because, remembering
how she touched
the man in the yard,
he could not look
at his wife's face,
Earl found himself alone
by the pump of the new
milking machine now out of breath,
or at a window of the barn.
Outside, where it was morning,
his father, the one-eyed man
with a cane, walked
to his old tractor
by turning himself back
to it and turning himself back
and back, as if he dragged
his body into this day
on the farm where nothing
seemed to move, even though
his father moved. And though
the cows, which had no idea
they were lifting their legs,
walked out of the barn,
and though his mother,
who had prayed this way
year after year, now stood
at the noon meal nodding

her head. Around her
the two hired men
closed their eyes,
and his father stared fast asleep
on one side of his face,
and Earl, who had never
seen them this way before,
thought of his wife
in the yard with the man
who sold him the machine.
He found again how she touched
the man's hands and chest,
and heard again as he watched
from the barn the milking machine's
great breathing. So
when he rose from the meal
with the rest, he could not go
to his home upstairs,
where she was. He walked
with his helpless father
closed away in his body,
and the hired men turning back
into the day, having no words
to say why nothing seemed
to move, though he himself
moved. And though he woke
from the thought of his wife

and the salesman and the machine's
great breath, to find himself
alone in the silo,
lifting his legs over
and over. Around him
as he packed with his feet,
the silage he had never seen
this way rained slowly
down from the high
chute, and the wood rose
so far and windowless,
Earl felt closed away
inside the great, stopped
farm forever. And all
he could hear in his body
that walked in the silo,
then back into the day,
was his own breath,
oh, the breath,
which now vanished
in the words he spoke
to the hired men, and left
in his long whistle
which brought the cows
with no idea it had brought them,
until he found himself alone
at the pump switch, unable

to breathe. Though all
around him in the dead barn,
with its locked cows,
the milking machine began
to make its sound over
and over, which seemed
to Earl like sighing,
like his lost breath.
He had no words to say why,
or why, when he looked
outside the barn window
and found his smiling wife
coming into the yard again,
and the salesman just
arriving in his new car, the whole
moving, breathing world seemed to him
suddenly outside. And so it was
that afternoon, he burst
open the stuck barn door
twisting its hinges,
and began to walk,
past his stopped, helpless
father, and past his mother,
who stood behind a screen window
in the house, calling his name,
until at last he reached
the two of them, backing slowly

away as they saw the pitchfork
he held in his hands.
He had no words
to tell them how far
he had come, or how much
he desired now to join them
with his whole body,
opening his lungs as if
for the first time to take breath.

The Town Museum

Maybe Davis lives alone
on his hill because
he found his wife
with her hand under the bib
of the hired man's bib
overalls, and maybe he speaks
to his mother in the perfectly
preserved room where she slept
and ate for twenty years,
and maybe he doesn't.
What we know is
that last spring when we looked
out of our picture windows
to find the source of all
the noise, it was Davis
at the wheel of his old
truck, too deaf to hear
he was in first gear,
and behind him a slow
semi, holding
a frail, swollen
sugarhouse like a soap bubble
on a wand. Maybe Davis is going
to tap the trees growing
in his fields, we said, or maybe
he is planning to take
the shrieking guinea hens

out of his trees
and put them in it;
but he wasn't.
Because the next time we looked,
the old cape from behind
the gas pumps was going right by
our pebble driveways, and then
an enormous, wasted
farmhouse, shutters
porch and all. Which was when
we called the selectman,
who just stood there
one hot day in July
watching old toothless
and shirtless Davis leading
the timbers and windows of somebody's
barn up his hill like pieces
of the last puzzle,
and who lifted
and flopped the baseball cap
back on his head and said maybe
it was some sort of
museum. What could you do
with such people, we said
across our new lawns
and kitchen bars, though
it turned out in the end he was

partly right. By this fall
when all the noise
stopped, Davis
had laid out one long
street of bent silos
and sagging sheds
and plastic-covered schoolhouse-
houses, which according to the meter-
reader, he watches from his porch
and sometimes even yells
out to. Lingering in our cars
these dark afternoons,
just back from Concord,
we think of crazy Davis
rocking and squinting
at the doors and windows
of nobody at all.
Maybe the sound
we hear, farther than wind
in our small trees,
is his voice,
high and breaking
over our roofs below.

Ghosts

When we went there,
the TV with the ghosts
would be on, and the father
talked and called out
every now and then to him,
sitting in that space
we always left around him,
Isn't it June? or Aren't
you June? And June
would laugh like only his voice
was doing it and he was somewhere
else, so when the father
turned back to us like
he was enjoying his son's
company, we could tell
he was on his way out,
too. Until at the end
he just sat saying nothing
all day into the dark.
Walking by there after chores,
we would see the blue light
from their TV, shifting
across the road in the trees,
and inside, those two dark
heads which had forgot
by this time even the cows.
So when the truck came

to take the manure-matted,
bellowing things to the slaughterhouse,
all we could say was, Thank God
for Liz. Who else
would have helped load them up,
then gone right on living
with that brother and father, dead
to the world in bib-overalls,
while all around them
the fields had begun
to forget they were fields?
Who else would have taken
that town job, punching
shoelace holes all night
into shoes? So now
when we went, there
would be Junior and his father
in the front room of the farm
they did not remember,
wearing brand-new shoes
they did not even know
they wore, watching the TV
with the ghosts. And there
would be Liz, with her apron on
over her pants, calling out
to them like they were only
deaf, Isn't it?

or Aren't you? and telling us
how at last they could have
no worries and be free.
And the thing was
that sometimes when we watched
them, watching those faces
which could no longer concentrate
on being faces, in the light
that shifted from news to ads
to sports, we could almost see
what she meant. But what
we didn't see was
that she also meant
herself. That the very
newspapers we sat on
each time we brought her milk
or eggs were Liz's own
slow way of forgetting all
her couches and chairs. Until
that last awful day
we went there,
after her father died,
and after the state car
came to take June,
and we found just flour-
bags and newspapers and Liz,
with her gray pigtail

coming undone, and no idea why
we'd left our rock-strewn fields
to come. Then all
we could think to do
was unplug that damned
TV, which by now didn't
have ghosts, only voices talking
beyond the continuous snow.
All we could do was
call her to come back
into her face and hands,
and Liz just watched
us, waving our arms,
like we weren't even there,
like we were the ghosts.

IV.

THE ABANDONMENT

To My Father, Dying in a Supermarket

At first it is difficult
to see you
are dropping dead—

you seem lost
in thought, adjusting your tie
as if to rehearse

some imaginary speech
though of course beginning
to fall,

your mouth opening wider
than I have ever seen
a mouth,

your hands deep
in your shirt,
going down

into the cheeses, making the sound
that is not
my name,

that explains nothing
over and over,
going away

into your hands
into your face,
leaving this great body

on its knees,
the father
of my body

which holds me
in this world,
watching you go

on falling
through the Musak,
making the sound

that is not my name,
that will never
explain anything, oh father,

stranger, all dressed up
and deserting me
for the last time.

My Brother Inside the Revolving Doors

I see you in Chicago, twenty-five years ago,
a tall kid, surprisingly sure of yourself.
You have just arrived from the goat farm
to meet your father, the god you invented
after he left you in childhood.
It is the sunniest day you can remember,
and you walk the wide streets
of the city by his side in the dream
you have had all along of this moment,
except you are beginning to see how different
he looks, and how he does not care
about this in the same way that you do.
Which is when it happens, you are taken
inside the doors. Just like that
you are shut off from him, walking
in the weightlessness of your own fear.
And when you push your door, it leads
to other retreating doors, and again
and again, it takes you to the voice of him,
the fat man standing outside who has nothing,
suddenly, to do with your father and shouts
let go! let go! and you cannot let go.

After My Stepfather's Death

Again it is the moment before I left home
for good, and my mother is sitting quietly
in the front seat while my stepfather pulls me
and my suitcase out of the car and begins
hurling my clothes, though now
I notice for the first time how the wind
unfolds my white shirt and puts its slow
arm in the sleeve of my blue shirt and lifts them
all into the air above our heads so beautifully
I want to shout at him to stop and look up
at what he has made, but of course when I turn
to him, a small man, bitter even this young
that the world will not go his way, my stepfather
still moves in his terrible anger, closing the trunk,
and closing himself into the car as hard as he can,
and speeding away into the last years of his life.

My Stepfather's Hands

All day in the sun
they have dreamed
of this amber room
behind half-drawn
blinds. Tenderly,
the hand with the weak
wrist turns each leaf
of the newspaper over
to the other one,
waiting to smooth it
under his eyes.
My stepfather's hands
have never been so happy.
Pieces of light stir
and float around them
in the not air, not water.

The Abandonment

Climbing on top of him and breathing
into his mouth this way she could be showing her
desire except that when she draws back
from him to make her little cries
she is turning to her young son just
coming into the room to find his father my brother
on the bed with his eyes closed and the slightest
smile on his lips as if when they
both beat on his chest as they do now
he will come back from the dream he is enjoying
so much he cannot hear her calling his name
louder and louder and the son saying get up
get up discovering both of them discovering
for the first time that all along
he has lived in this body this thing
with shut lids dangling its arms
that have nothing to do with him and everything
they can ever know the wife listening weeping
at his chest and the mute son who will never
forget how she takes the face into her hands now
as if there were nothing in the world
but the face and breathes oh
breathes into the mouth which does not breathe back.

String

If his last, knotted
words, this string

of thought could be undone,
if you could loosen

each frayed curse
against his life, untie

and unloop the *must*
and *will* of every

secret promise,
and ravel up page

by page the night
after night of all

he wrote, to put it safely
back into the hand

of this man everyone
now says lived

only for his family,
and built a breezeway,

deck and bar, and each
day gave everything

he had to his work,
you might never guess

these words,
this string,

how much there was
to bind him up

and hold him still.

V.

THE REVIVAL

A Traveler's Advisory

The main streets of towns
don't go uphill,
and the houses aren't
purple like that
tenement with one eye
clapboarded over. Never mind
how it wavers
backward, watching you
try to find second gear.
You've arrived
at the top of the town:
a closed garage
where nobody's dog
sits, collarless,
and right next door
a church which seems
to advertise Unleaded.
Who's hung this
great front door
above no steps? No one
you'd know.
And what suspends
the avalanche
of barn? Nothing,
and you will never

escape the bump,
lifting shiny with tar.
And you won't
need the sign that says
you are leaving Don't Blink,
Can't Dance,
or Town of No.

Seeing Cooch

Most winter days,
passing that
wreck of a house
all wrapped
in plastic,
you do not
find him. It just
sits by the ramp
to 89 like
a great loaf
of bread. Yet
there are times
just before
your mind closes
on the traffic
toward Concord, you see
the slow, black
coat of Cooch.
He will be out
on his failed
porch, studying
a tire or something
without a drawer.
Some nights you see him
in a room beyond
his plastic-covered
windows, moving
in the afterlife
of ruined things.

Hunt Walking

If you could be there
with the rest, coming out

of Vernondale's store
on this hot day

in spring, and if,
looking far down the road

where the white houses waver
in heat, you could see

for the first time
since winter, old Hunt,

the crippled man, walking
by not quite falling

down first on one side,
then on the other

holding aloft the bony
wing of his cane,

you would understand why
they have stopped

on the porch by the sign
that says Yes We Are Open,

without knowing
where they are

going, or what it is
they hold in their hands.

The Minister's Death

That long fall,
when the voices stopped
in the tweed mouth
of his radio, and sermons
stood behind the door
of his study in files
no one would ever again inspect,
and even the black shoes
and vestments, emptied of him,
were closed away,
they sat together Sundays
in the house, now hers—
the son wearing his suit
and water-combed hair,
and mother in a housedress,
holding the dead
man's cane. Somewhere
at the edge of the new
feeling just beginning
between them, floorlamps
bloomed triple bulbs
and windowsills sagged
with African violets,
and the old woman,
not knowing exactly how
to say his face looked lovely
in the chair, encircled

by a white aura
of doily, said nothing
at all. And the son,
not used to feeling
small inside the great
shoulderpads of his suit,
looked down at the rugs
on rugs to where the trees kept
scattering the same, soft
puzzle of sunlight
until, from time to time,
she found the words
of an old dialogue they both
could speak: "How has the weather
been this week? What time
did you start out from Keene?"

The Revival

What was she to do
when the life came back
into her foot and leg,
and her arm remained a thing
that slipped down into
the wheelchair—what
but lift it out
with her well hand,
and flop it back
into her lap over
and over. Each visit
while we talked,
she carried on her wordless
conversation, patting it
and showing it how to bend
and bend, then holding it
to her breast, poor
retarded baby. Poor Mother,
prostrated in blouses
bought for the trip
she never got to take,
pulling the fingers up
from the eggless nest
of that palm, and staring
at it, just as she did
the night her arm
suddenly moved—

floated, wobbling
up into the light,
dangling the hand like
seaweed from the depths
of its strange sleep.
And then, above the shining
chrome bars of the bed,
it paused to turn
its wrist, until
we saw the miracle
was not the arm, but she
who held it there,
and spoke only to herself
in her small voice
about the mysterious power
she'd found to raise
it up, asking again
and again, "What do you
know about that?"

Sue Reed Walking

Cupboard dishes jerk past
her head,
family portraits,

colored photographs
of Keene. She is looking
straight down, amazed

by her left leg struggling
against a current
she cannot see. O

she doesn't know
when her glasses flash
up from that depth

quite where she is,
or that her sweater
twists childishly

behind her back
but never mind.
And never mind her hair

is matted
and her stiff hand
carries its useless

puff of air.
Note with what care
she places her three–

pronged cane to pull herself
back together again
and again. Listen

to her warn the cat
"I'm coming through!"
Watch Sue Reed, walking.

Happiness

Why, Dot asks, stuck in the back
seat of her sister's two-door, her freckled hand
feeling the roof for the right spot
to pull her wide self up onto her left,
the unarthritic, ankle—why
does her sister, coaching outside on her cane,
have to make her laugh so, she flops
back just as she was, though now
looking wistfully out through the restaurant
reflected in her back window, she seems bigger,
and couldn't possibly mean we should go
ahead in without her, she'll be all right, and so
when you finally place the pillow behind her back
and lift her right out into the sunshine,
all four of us are happy, none more
than she, who straightens the blossoms
on her blouse, says how nice it is to get out
once in awhile, and then goes in to eat
with the greatest delicacy (oh
I could never finish all that) and aplomb
the complete roast beef dinner with apple crisp
and ice cream, just a small scoop.

The Visit

We were at the camp, it must have been
some afternoon that summer
when your Aunt Rose came back
from her stroke, because her mouth
looked skeptical, almost provocative,
as if she had suddenly achieved the role
of the great lady she'd spent a lifetime
preparing for. And I remember how,
with this new dignity, she turned
to Uncle Bert's thought about the good
taste of beer on a hot day as if
he weren't wearing Bermuda shorts
and wing-tipped shoes at all,
but a loincloth. How could he
have known that she meant, if he waited
a few respectful minutes, just one
would be OK, and what was more
(the porch had got so hot, even
with the breeze), Aunt Rose would feel
compelled to have one too? So,
what Bert came back with was beers
for everybody, even Rose's 80-
year-old sister, do you remember,
the one who was shrinking and said Oh,
because she liked the cheese
your mother brought out or the small flowers
on the TV tray or the wind that threatened

to blow her wide hat off? It didn't,
of course, and when Rose said No, no, no,
Bertram, we knew he could go on telling
what they did when they were younger,
because it had turned out to be
one of those wonderful days which had nothing
quite to do with wind or words. So Bert
just sat there, his white legs happy
to be free of pants, and talked—was it
about the wildest party, or how fast they drove
in his new car afterward? And while
they said they couldn't stay, they stayed
until the last light rose into the tops
of the trees around us on the lake,
and the wind suddenly stopped,
and even Aunt Rose said how nice
it had got. Perfection
is what almost doesn't happen.

What It Is

It is not what,
carrying that
afterthought of legs,
he runs to, and not
what his interrogative, foldy
face detects
on the floor, because
it is always changing, always
turning out to be
some other bug
or bush his nose wanted,
leaving his tail
smoldering
behind, and
it is never,
after all that scratching
and lifting of leg,
enough: not even
after he joins
the dinner party, smiling
upside-down
and rolling
his testicles, not even
in his whimpering sleep,
dreaming in the tips
of his paws
that he is chasing

it, that very thing
which, scratching,
he can't quite
reach, nor sniffing find,
because in the perfect
brainlessness of dog,
he will never know
what it is.

When Paul Flew Away

It was the same as always,
Paul opening the big, black lung
of it with that worried look
while the cats watched
from under the stove,
but when he closed
his eyes and begun to sink
down between the straps
of his bib overalls,
it was like he died. Except
the accordion was still breathing
a waltz between his hands,
except he called back
to us every so often
from wherever he was, Shit.
Which meant everything
he had ever known
in his life up to that
moment, but this song.
Not some sock-drawer
music of getting a tune out
and then rummaging
for the chord to match,
but together, exactly like
he was breathing the thing
himself. No stomping
either, just Paul twisting

like he was after some deep
itch, only right then
he was starting to lift
out of his chair. Slowly
at first, like flypaper
in a small breeze, then
the whole enormous weight
of him hanging over the sink. God,
he was happy, and I
and the kids was laughing
and happy, when all
at once it come to me,
this is it. Paul is leaving
the old Barcolounger
stuck in second
position, and the TV on top
of the TV that don't
work, and all my hand-paintings
of strawberries as if he never
said this would be Strawberry Farm.
Hey! I said out in the yard
because he was already going
right over the roof
of the goat-shed, pumping
that song. What about you
and me? And Paul
just got farther and smaller

until he looked like a kid
unfolding paper dolls over
and over, or like
he was clapping slowly
at himself, and then
like he was opening up the wings
of some wild, black bird
he had made friends with
just before he disappeared
into the sky above the clouds
over all of Wisconsin.

The Man With The Radios

Beyond the curtainless
bay windows of his room
on the side street,

he kneels
among old radios, left
from a time of belief

in radios,
some dangling fat
tails of cord

from end tables, some
in darkening corners
sprouting hairs of wire

from their great backs,
and this strange one
he has chosen,

standing on the paws
of an African cat.
The man with the radios

is so far away
in his gaze you would swear
he hears nothing,

so still you might miss
how he concentrates
on not moving

his hand. Slowly,
slowly he turns
its ridged

knob in the dark,
listening for the sound
he has prepared it for,

watching with his absent eyes
the film that clears
from a green eye.

About the Author

Wesley McNair's work has appeared in numerous national magazines and anthologies. His first book, *The Faces of Americans in 1853*, won the Devins Award for Poetry. He has also received a Guggenheim Fellowship in poetry, two grants from the National Endowment for the Arts, the Pushcart Prize, and the Eunice Tietjens Prize from *Poetry* magazine. He is currently a professor in the creative writing program at the University of Maine at Farmington, and lives in Mercer, Maine.

THE TOWN OF NO

was set on the Linotron 202 in Bembo, a design based on the types used by Venetian scholar-publisher Aldus Manutius in the printing of *De Aetna*, written by Pietro Bembo and published in 1495. The original characters were cut in 1490 by Francesco Griffo who, at Aldus's request, later cut the first italic types. Originally adapted by the English Monotype Company, Bembo is now widely available and highly regarded. It remains one of the most elegant, readable, and widely used of all book faces.

Composed by DEKR Corporation, Woburn, Massachusetts. Printed and bound by Haddon Craftsmen, Scranton, Pennsylvania. Designed by Lucinda L. Hitchcock.